All children have a strong desire to read to themselves...

and a sense of achievement when they can do so. The **read it yourself** *series has been devised to satisfy their desire, and to give them that sense of achievement. The series is graded for specific reading ages, using simple vocabulary and sentence structure, and the illustrations complement the text so that the words and pictures together form an integrated whole.*

LADYBIRD BOOKS, INC.
Lewiston, Maine 04240 U.S.A.

Loughborough, Leicestershire, England

Printed in England

Rapunzel

adapted by Fran Hunia
from the traditional tale
illustrated by Kathie Layfield

Ladybird Books

A man and his wife
look into a witch's garden.

They see some lettuce.

''That lettuce looks good,''
says the woman.

''Yes,'' says the man.
''I will get some for you.''

''No,'' says his wife.
''It is the witch's lettuce.
We can't have any.''

The woman keeps
looking at the lettuce.
She wants it very much.

Soon she starts to get ill.

"I will have to get
some lettuce for you,"
says the man.

The man climbs
into the witch's garden
and gets some lettuce.

He takes it home
and gives it to his wife.

She is pleased
with the lettuce.

The man climbs
into the witch's garden
again.

The witch is waiting.

She sees the man
take some lettuce.

"That's *my* lettuce,"
she says. "Give it back."

"Please let me have it,"
says the man.
"I want it for my wife.
She is ill."

The witch says,
"You can have the lettuce,
but when your wife
has a baby,
you must give it to me.
I will give the baby
a good home."

One day the woman
has a baby girl, Rapunzel.

The witch comes to get her.

"Come with me, Rapunzel,"
she says.

The man and his wife
have to give Rapunzel
to the witch.

The witch takes
Rapunzel away.

She keeps her in a tower.

Rapunzel can't get down,
and she has no one
to talk to.

When the witch
wants to see Rapunzel,
she goes to the tower
and says,
"Rapunzel, Rapunzel,
let down your hair."

Rapunzel lets her hair down
to the witch.

The witch climbs up
Rapunzel's hair
and goes into the tower.

One day a prince
rides by the tower.

He hears Rapunzel singing.

He looks for her,
but he can't see her,
and he can't get
into the tower.

He goes home.

The prince wants
to see Rapunzel.

He goes back to the tower.

When the witch comes,
she doesn't see the prince.

She says,
''Rapunzel, Rapunzel,
let down your hair.''

The prince hears.

The prince sees Rapunzel
let her hair down.

He sees the witch
climb up it
and go into the tower.

The prince waits
for the witch to climb down
Rapunzel's hair
and go home.

He goes to the tower
and says,
"Rapunzel, Rapunzel,
let down your hair."

Rapunzel lets her hair down.

The prince climbs up it,
and goes into the tower.

Rapunzel is pleased
to see him.

They talk and talk.

When the prince
is about to go, he says,
''Can I come and see you
again, Rapunzel?''

''Yes,'' says Rapunzel.

The prince comes to see
Rapunzel again and again.

One day he says,
''Please marry me, Rapunzel.''

''I want to marry you,''
says Rapunzel,
''but we can't get married
here in this tower.
I will have to get down.
Can you help me?''

The prince says
he will help.

"Please get me some silk,"
says Rapunzel.
"I will make a ladder
so that I can climb down."

The prince gets some silk
for Rapunzel.

He takes it to the tower
and says,
"Rapunzel, Rapunzel,
let down your hair."

Rapunzel lets her hair down.

The prince climbs up
and gives her the silk.

Rapunzel starts
to make a ladder.

One day the witch
comes to see Rapunzel.

She hurts Rapunzel's hair
when she climbs up it.

Rapunzel says,
"The prince doesn't hurt me
when he climbs up my hair."

The witch is angry.

She cuts Rapunzel's hair
and takes her away.

The witch
waits in the tower
for the prince to come.

The prince comes
to the tower
and calls,
''Rapunzel, Rapunzel,
let down your hair.''

The witch has
Rapunzel's hair.

She lets it down
to the prince.

The prince climbs up
Rapunzel's hair.

He looks for Rapunzel,
but she isn't there.

When he sees the witch,
he jumps down.

The prince hurts his eyes when he jumps down.

He can't see.

He walks away.

The prince walks on and on.

One day he hears
a girl singing.

It is Rapunzel.

The prince goes to her.

Rapunzel is so happy
to see the prince
that she starts to cry.

Her tears fall
on the prince's eyes.

The prince can see again.

Rapunzel goes home
with the prince,
and they get married.